WHITE RIVER WOLVES

JOSIE'S MIRACLE

DAWN SULLIVAN

Published by Dawn Sullivan

Cover Design: Kari Ayasha-Cover to Cover Designs

Photographer: Mandy Hollis Photography

Model: Randi Sue

Language: English

Merry Christmas to all of my readers. It has been a wonderful journey so far. Thanks for coming along for the ride!

The wolf ran swiftly through the layers of fresh, soft, beautiful white snow that covered the vast landscape owned by the White River Wolves. Her stunning russet colored coat with patches of white and black throughout was covered with snow. Small icicles clung to the fur on her stomach. The wolf, Josie Bennett, was the doctor for the White River Wolves; as their doctor, she had an obligation to the pack. It had been weeks since she allowed herself the pleasure of changing into her wolf form and simply running free. It was not often that she was able to take advantage of the simple joys in life, but tonight she could not resist.

Josie loved everything about winter. She loved the cold, crisp air and the feel of the light, fluffy snow slipping through her paws as she ran. She loved going home, curling up in front of the fire with a cup of hot chocolate and snuggling in with a new romance novel. She was a romantic at heart and enjoyed reading about the heroes and heroines getting their happily ever after. She always dreamed her time would come, but as the years went by without Josie finding love and happiness, she gradually stopped hoping. Now her life was centered on her work, and there was little time for anything else.

Christmas was Josie's favorite holiday. She could not believe it was only a couple of weeks away. She always made sure the hospital she was in charge of had a large Christmas tree in the outer waiting area with lights, ornaments, and a huge angel adorning the top. The entire hospital was decorated with garland, lights and bows. In the hospital gardens there was a Nativity scene featuring the three wise men, Joseph, the Virgin Mary, and baby Jesus. Every tree in front of, and surrounding, the hospital was adorned with brightly colored Christmas lights.

Josie enlisted the help of other pack members with the majority of the decorating, but there was one tradition she always made time for. The month before Christmas, she went shopping and made sure every child in the White River wolf pack had a special gift. It took a full weekend of nonstop shopping to get everything she needed, but it was worth it.

On Christmas Eve, the parents brought their children to the hospital. Chase Montgomery, the pack alpha, dressed up as Santa Claus and handed out the gifts to the children. It had been a tradition for several years, and was something Josie looked forward to each year.

Lost in thought, Josie almost missed the faint whimpering noise. Stopping, she perked her ears forward, listening intently, and inhaled deeply. There, she heard it again. It was a child; one in pain. She slipped through the woods quietly, cringing when the smell of the child's fear became rancid in the air. Josie was a couple of miles from home and the immediate safety of the pack. There was no reason for a child to be this far out without supervision. Especially not this late at night.

Wondering briefly if it could be a trap of some kind, Josie cautiously followed the faint noise of the child's crying. The sound drew her even further away from town. She knew she should go back and find help, but the thought of a helpless child in need pushed her forward.

Inhaling deeply, Josie caught the scent of the small bear cub named Hunter. Hunter came to live with the pack several months ago. His adopted father, Phoenix, was a member of RARE. RARE, Rescue and Retrieval Extractions, was an elite team of mercenaries that were called in to find and rescue kidnapping victims. There was no way Phoenix would allow his cub to wander off this far from home.

"Shut up you sniveling little brat," a male voice ordered. "I am going to get a lot of money for you." Money? Josie had no idea who the man was, and she didn't care. No one was going to sell that little boy. Slowly and silently, Josie stalked the man who was in the process of kidnapping Hunter. She was a doctor and had sworn an oath to save lives; however, there was a child in danger. She was not above inflicting some damage to save a child.

Hearing a grunt and loud curse, Josie slipped around a tree and snuck up behind the man who was holding the small child by his throat. Hunter was gasping for breath as the man held him suspended off the ground. "Kick me again, and I will kill you," the man snarled. Pulling back a fist, he started to swing it at Hunter's head. Josie was on him before the punch connected. Anger consumed her at the sight of Hunter being held helplessly by his throat, three feet off the ground, and she unleashed her fury full force on the man.

Dropping Hunter, the kidnapper let out a vicious snarl as he tried to fight off Josie. He pummeled her with his fists and struck out with a foot, but she felt nothing beyond the anger controlling her. Hell-bent on destroying the man, Josie sank her teeth into his body again and again, her back claws tearing into his jean clad legs. She had him down on the ground within minutes, her jaws wrapped tightly around his throat.

The sound of sobbing slowly brought Josie out of her deep rage. Carefully, she removed her teeth and backed away from what was left of the man. He was still alive, but barely. There were cuts and lacerations all over his body where Josie had torn through his thick layers of clothing and found skin. Blood pooled on the ground around him. A part of her, the part that said she was a doctor first and foremost, wanted to save him. To sew up his wounds and give the man back his life. But another sob from Hunter sealed his fate. Children would always come first. She needed to get Hunter home to his family.

Tentatively, Josie approached the boy. Lying down beside him, she nuzzled him gently with her nose. Whining softly, she licked his cheek and yipped quietly. Opening his eyes, he watched her warily though his tears. "Doc Josie," he whispered, reaching out and slipping his freezing cold fingers into her fur. The child was obviously in shock and emotionally shutting down.

Josie wanted to change into her human form, snatch the little boy up, and cuddle him close. Unfortunately, she could not because she did not have any clothes nearby. She had removed her clothing and changed into her wolf form at her house, leaving through the special door installed on her back porch.

Hunter was shaking from fear and the cold. She had to get him home quickly. Gently nudging him with her nose again, she coaxed him to stand up so they could get moving. Struggling to his feet, Hunter cried out and more tears escaped as he collapsed back onto the ground. That was when Josie noticed the blood flowing from his leg. It looked as if it had been sliced open. There was no way he could walk with that injury.

Turning swiftly, Josie ran back to where the man lay taking his last breaths. Shifting into her human form, Josie quickly removed the coat from his body. The last thing she wanted to do was have this evil man's stench on her, but she had no choice. Shrugging into the heavy coat, she zipped it up and tugged the bottom of it down as far as it would go. It just barely covered her thighs, but it would have to do.

Rushing over to Hunter, she quickly gathered him in her arms and started to run back toward town. Instead of going to Hunter's home, Josie decided to take him directly to the hospital where she could sew up his leg. Running as fast as she could, her bare feet slipping and sliding through the snow, Josie gripped the boy tighter in her arms. She blocked out the pain and discomfort in her feet from the icy snow and pushed forward. Her need to keep the child safe overrode her own fear.

Reaching town, Josie moved quickly to the hospital. Entering the front doors, she thought briefly of the sight she must make. All she wore was a dead man's coat that stopped several inches above her knees, and she was obviously naked underneath it. The coat was covered in rips and tears, and was saturated with blood. After the fight she had been in, she was sure her body was covered in blood, also. Her feet were bright red and raw from running more than two miles in the cold snow, and she was carrying an unconscious little boy who had blood dripping from one leg. Thankfully, Hunter had lost consciousness on the last mile of their journey.

As the nurse at the front desk stared in shock, Josie ordered, "I need a room and some scrubs. Get the alpha and Phoenix Madison here, now." Hurrying past her, Josie moved to the first empty room. Placing Hunter down on the bed, she removed his shoes and pants, issuing orders to the two nurses who had immediately followed her into the room. The cut was deep enough that it would definitely need stitches.

Grabbing the scrubs a nurse held out to her, Josie ordered them to clean the wound while she changed. Ignoring the people in the room, Josie quickly pulled on the pants, then stripped off the coat and threw it in the trashcan.

After slipping on the top, she moved to the sink on the far side of the room. Wetting a paper towel, she scrubbed her face quickly to remove the blood. When she was done, she washed her hands and arms in scalding hot water, before drying them and putting on surgical gloves.

Moving back over to Hunter, Josie smiled gently when she realized his eyes were open and he was watching her. The fear was still there, but the pure terror had faded into something more manageable. "Hey, little man," she murmured, as she checked the wound to make sure it was cleaned properly. "I am going to give you a shot to numb the area around your wound. Then I am going to put in some stitches. You will get to show them off to all of your friends." Flashing Hunter a grin, Josie continued to talk, hopefully distracting him as she numbed the area. Sparing him another quick glance, she saw Hunter's eyes fixed on what she was doing. Deciding he was going to be all right, she began to stitch the six-inch gash closed.

"What happened, Hunter?" she asked quietly while she worked. The wound was a knife wound, the clean swipe meant to stun and distract, making it so the child could not shift.

A tear rolled down Hunter's cheek, but he didn't answer, fear keeping him silent. She had seen it before and did not push. He would talk when he was ready.

Josie heard a commotion in the doorway just as she was finishing up. Looking over, she saw Chase, Phoenix, and Serenity enter the room. "We are almost done here," she told them, as she tied off the last stitch. Removing the latex gloves, she tossed them in the trash. Reaching out, Josie ran her fingers through the young boy's hair. Smiling, she said, "Hunter did great. I think we might have a doctor in the making here."

Hunter smiled weakly, a soft sob escaping him when Serenity ran forward and enveloped him in her arms. "I can heal you, sweetie," Serenity said, moving her hand down his leg.

Catching a distinct scent that she had not noticed before, Josie grabbed Serenity's hand before it could connect with the wound. "No, you are not healing him, Serenity." Serenity turned to Josie with a low, menacing growl. Opening her mouth, Serenity flashed her fangs. Serenity was gifted with the ability to heal with the touch of her hand. Josie was interfering with Serenity's ability by not allowing her to heal her son, and she was not happy.

Before Josie could respond, another deep growl rolled across the room. A large man shoved his way through the people crowding the entrance of the doorway and moved to where Josie stood. Slipping an arm in front of her, he gently pushed her back behind him as he bared his teeth in Serenity's direction. This pissed Phoenix off, and there was a hell of a lot of growling after that, but Josie ignored it all. Standing behind the male defending her, she closed her eyes and breathed in deeply, inhaling his scent. A soft moan escaped her lips before she could hold it back. God, he smelled so good; spicy, musky, with a hint of cinnamon. He was here. After all these years, Josie had finally found her mate.

Vaguely, Josie was aware of Chase trying to get control of the situation, but she was having trouble concentrating. Reaching out, she lightly touched her mate's back, eyes widening when she felt the powerful muscles bunch under her hand. Sliding her fingertips down, she moaned again as a shudder of desire rippled through her. Feeling her own fangs fighting to break through so that she could sink them into the man's neck, claiming him, Josie swallowed hard and fought to regain control. The growling in the room escalated and finally the noise penetrated the sensual fog in Josie's mind.

Pulling her hand away, Josie stepped around her mate and loudly ordered, "Stop this right now. All of you." Under her stern gaze and no-nonsense tone, the room finally quieted. Her mate stepped up behind her, pulling her back against his body and lightly resting a protective hand on her hip. Josie shivered at the last small growl that vibrated through his chest.

Turning to Serenity, she apologized. "I'm sorry, Serenity. I know you want to help your son, but you can't in your condition. We don't know what it will do to the baby you are carrying. I cannot allow you to endanger your baby when Hunter is going to be fine. He has stitches and I will give him medicine to help with the pain. In a couple of days he can shift to speed up the healing process."

Serenity's eyes widened in wonder, and she covered her stomach protectively with one hand. Her eyes filling with tears, she whispered, "Baby?" Her shocked gaze sought out Phoenix. "We are having a baby?"

A wide grin split across Phoenix's face. Crossing the room, he slipped his arms around Serenity, nuzzling her neck. "Your scent changed recently, but I didn't realize what it meant." Stroking a hand down her long hair, he tilted her head and kissed her lovingly on the lips. "It's best to listen to Doc Josie on this, sweetheart. We don't know if your gift could hurt the baby."

Nodding, Serenity leaned into Phoenix and then pulled Hunter closer to her. "I am so sorry, honey. I would heal you if I could."

Hunter snuggled closer to Serenity and closed his eyes. "It's okay, Mama," he said with a tired sigh. "Doc Josie fixed it. She always does. Except for the bad guy. She didn't fix him." Another sigh escaped him as he drifted off to sleep.

In the silence that followed, everyone turned from Hunter to Josie. Her mate's hand tightened on her hip before letting go. He backed up to the wall, resting casually against it. Surprised that he let her go, she turned curiously in his direction. That was when she got her first good look at the man that would be hers for the rest of her life. He was tall with broad shoulders, and a stocky, muscular build. Dark brown hair fell in curls on his forehead and over his ears, above deep chocolate brown eyes.

Her eyes widened as she inhaled again. A bear. Her mate was a bear. Josie always thought if she did find her mate, he would be a wolf, like her. Not that she was complaining. Her bear was gorgeous, and the protectiveness in him warmed her heart.

Some shifters looked their whole lives for their mate and never found them. Some gave up and instead settled for love and a family. Josie was so focused on her career that she didn't have time to look for love or a relationship. She had always secretly hoped she would find her mate, the other half of her soul. As the years passed, she slowly gave up on that dream, and instead threw herself into her job, dedicating her life to her pack. Now, when she least expected it, he was here.

His eyes never left Josie. Self-consciously, she remembered what she must look like. Avoiding her mate's gaze, she ran a tired hand through her long brown waves and cringed when she felt the dried blood stuck in the strands. Walking over to a mirror above the sink, Josie gasped at the vision she made. There were still dried specs of blood on her face and neck, not to mention what was stuck in her hair. Turning on the water, Josie ignored the others as she frantically started scrubbing the blood off her skin. She was horrified she just met her mate looking the way she did.

"Josie," Chase's voice interrupted her thoughts. Josie

ignored him as she started cleaning the blood off her chin. Tears filled her eyes as her thoughts went back to the reason that the blood was there. She killed a man. She, Doctor Josie Bennett, the woman who had promised to uphold an oath to always save lives, killed a man. Shaking uncontrollably, Josie cried out when she felt hands on her shoulders. Yanking away, she swung around to confront whoever had touched her. She quickly lowered her eyes to the floor and bared her neck when she realized it was her alpha.

"Stop, Josie," Chase said, as he lightly put his arms around her and pulled her closer. When her mate's growl once more filled the room, Josie pulled out of Chase's comforting arms.

"What in the hell is wrong with you, Ryker?" a female voice broke in as a petite, slender woman entered the room. She had long dark hair with burgundy highlights and flashing silver eyes. Stopping in front of Josie's mate, she slid her hands to her hips and demanded, "What's your problem?"

As much as Josie wanted to tear into the woman for talking to her mate the way she was, she just did not have the energy. Ryker, she corrected herself. His name was Ryker.

The night was catching up with her and Josie just wanted to go home, shower, and crawl into bed. Unfortunately, that was not going to happen anytime soon. First, she needed to tell everyone what had taken place out in the woods.

"Back off, Storm," Ryker bit out, his eyes cold and hard. "You are my partner, not my keeper." Ignoring Storm, Ryker turned his full attention back to Josie.

"What happened?" he demanded. "Where did all of that blood come from?"

Partner, Josie thought distractedly. What exactly did Ryker do? Scanning his tall, muscular body, Josie noticed a gun strapped to his waist and another one on his leg. She caught the glint of a blade from a knife tucked into a side holster. He has to be an enforcer, she decided. Pairing an enforcer with a doctor. Fate had some funny ideas sometimes.

Taking in Josie's stiff posture, pure white face, and trembling fingers, Ryker left the wall he was leaning against and walked over to where she stood. Gently, he removed the wet paper towel from her shaking hand. "Talk to me, Mate," Ryker urged quietly. His mate. His beautiful, sexy mate. Ryker was an enforcer for the shifter council. He didn't have time for a mate, and he definitely did not need the distraction of one. But one look into Josie's beautiful dark brown eyes, one touch of her soft, silky skin, one whiff of her intoxicating scent, and he was gone. Attraction was instant for mates and he was hard as hell and wanting to be alone with Josie now. Screw the council and the mission. He had a mate to claim.

Ignoring the shocked gasp that came from Storm, Ryker continued to wipe away the dried blood from the underside of Josie's chin. Damn, she was breathtaking. Slipping a chestnut curl behind her ear, he gently cupped Josie's cheek and stroked his thumb along her full, soft lips. Groaning, he just barely held himself back from claiming those sexy, plump lips with his own.

Hearing Chase clear his throat behind them, Ryker decided they needed to hurry this discussion along so that he could find out who he needed to kill, and then get Josie home to take care of her.

Tugging on her hand, Ryker led Josie over to a chair on the far side of the room by a window. Sitting down, he pulled her onto his lap and stroked a calming hand down her arm as he hugged her close. When she moved her small, soft bottom over his erection, he realized sitting in the chair might not have been his smartest move. Burying his face in her neck, he fought for control of his body.

Chase followed them to the chair and knelt down beside Josie. "Congratulations, Josie," he told her with a smile. "If I'd known Ryker was your mate, I would have introduced you when he was here months ago."

Josie glanced at him in surprise. Looking back and forth between Chase and Ryker, she asked, "He's been here before?"

Several months ago, Ryker thought. He had been here eight months ago. Not once had he seen this gorgeous woman on any of his visits. Even if he had seen her from a distance, he would have remembered.

"Ryker is an enforcer for the shifter council, Josie." Chase informed her. "He was here when Lily was taken in April, and he was beneficial in the rescue of several women the General held at different facilities." The alpha's niece, Lily, was kidnapped by a sadistic bastard known as the General at the end of April. Not only had RARE been called in to find Lily, but the shifter council had also been involved. Ryker had been to the White

River compound several times, but not once had he seen or scented Josie. If he had, she would not be unclaimed right now.

"Josie," Chase continued. "We need you to tell us what happened to you and Hunter. If there is someone out there running free on our lands, I need to send our enforcers out to track them down and bring them back. I need to know what we are dealing with."

Ryker felt Josie stiffen in his arms. Swallowing hard, she whispered, "I understand, Alpha." Straightening up in Ryker's lap, Josie clasped her hands tightly together and ducked her head so her waves of dark hair covered her face. Refusing to allow her to hide from him, Ryker slid a hand through her hair and fisted it at the back of her head. Forcing her to meet his gaze, he nodded for her to continue.

Her eyes never leaving his, Josie started. "I was out running. I have been so busy I haven't been on a real run in weeks, but I couldn't resist the snow tonight. About two miles out I heard Hunter. He was crying and a man was yelling at him." She stopped as Phoenix interrupted them with a snarl.

Tightening his hold in her hair, Ryker brought her gaze back to him. "Go on," he encouraged.

Glancing back at Phoenix in concern, Josie continued. "I snuck up on them as quickly as I could. When I reached them, the man was holding Hunter off the ground, his hand wrapped around the cub's neck. I don't remember much after that. My wolf went crazy at the sight of Hunter being hurt. The man is...dead."

Staring at Josie in stunned surprise, Ryker tried to grasp the fact that she had actually killed a man. He had the feeling she was normally a strong, confident woman, but she was not a killer. She was a doctor, a healer. Knowing she had taken a life must be tearing her up inside. Ryker wished he had killed the bastard instead.

"I need you to show us where you left him, Josie," Chase told her. When Josie cringed, Ryker felt a protective growl escape. "Point us in the right direction," Chase coaxed. "If you give us the vicinity of where you left the body, we can track it."

"I can do that," Josie agreed with a short nod. "I can do better. I shifted so that I could carry Hunter here. There was no way he was walking on that leg. I needed clothes, so I wore the man's coat. You can use it to track him when you get near."

Ryker had wondered what the subtle smell was that surrounded his mate. It was a good thing the cold air must have muted the scent, because his bear was going crazy at the idea of Josie wearing anything that belonged to another man.

"Let me get Serenity and Hunter home, and we will track the bastard down. Give me twenty minutes. I'm calling in RARE," Phoenix said, as he scooped the sleeping Hunter up in his arms. "Can you send a couple of enforcers over to protect my family while I am gone?"

"Of course," Chase agreed, rising from where he had been squatting on the floor. "I will send Aiden and Xavier over now. Let me know what you find out."

"You aren't coming?" Phoenix asked in surprise. The attempted kidnapping had taken place on White River land. Normally, as alpha, Chase would be the first to arrive at the scene.

"Angel will be there," Chase said, as he made his way to the door. "One alpha is sufficient."

Angel was the leader of RARE, and the alpha of their group. The team would not answer to anyone but her. Angel was also Chase's mate, even though they had not completed the mate bond yet.

Ryker did not know the specifics, but he did know that for some reason Angel was holding back. He was sure part of the reason Chase was relinquishing control to her now was because he did not want to face her. Having a mate, but not bonding with them, could slowly drive a shifter insane. It had been eight months since Chase and Angel met. Ryker was surprised they had held out this long.

"Let me know as soon as you have any answers. Make sure to dispose of the body." Looking back over his shoulder at Ryker, Chase asked, "You will see that Josie gets home safely?" Ryker nodded. Of course, he would take care of his mate. "I'll send Slade and Charlotte to shadow Josie for a few days while you are gone in Denver." Chase said. "They will be there within the hour."

Shit, his mission. The whole reason he was even in Colorado. Ryker and Storm were sent to Denver to hunt down a pack of rogue wolf shifters that had recently kidnapped a young female fox shifter from Minnesota. They stopped in to briefly explain the situation to Chase and ask him to have his people keep their eyes and ears open. When a nurse called Chase and told him it looked like their doctor and Hunter were attacked, Ryker had been curious and followed Chase to the hospital.

After finding Josie, he did not want to go to Denver,

but no matter how much Ryker wanted to stay with her, he had a duty to the council and the fox shifter.

After Chase left, Josie gave Phoenix directions to the spot where she left the dead man. Phoenix collected the man's coat from the trashcan where Josie tossed it earlier, then took his family home.

In the silence that followed, Ryker tried to figure out how to explain to Josie that he had to put his duty to the council over his own mate. Sighing deeply, he rested his forehead against her shoulder.

"I can go on without you, Ryker," Storm offered. "You get Josie settled in and come to Denver tomorrow. I should have some intel by then."

"No," Ryker ground out, raising his head to glare at Storm. It was their mission. As much as he wanted to stay with Josie, he had pledged himself to the council and he needed to see this through. "Give me time to get Josie home and make sure she is safe, and then we will head out."

Josie shifted on his lap, making his rock-hard erection even harder, if that were possible. He wanted nothing more than to sink into her balls deep, but now was not the time. Lightly messaging the back of her head where his hand still rested, he continued, "Call our contacts in Denver and see what you can find out, Storm. Meet me at the truck in an hour."

Lifting an eyebrow, Storm asked sarcastically, "You think that will be long enough?"

Pissed off with Storm's attitude, Ryker briefly let his bear show through, the tips of his fangs peeking out as he growled.

Eyes widening, Storm backed toward the door, hands

held out in a placating manner. "See you in an hour," she smirked before turning and sauntering out the door.

Finally, everyone was gone. Ryker was done waiting. He needed to taste his mate now. Fisting his hand in Josie's hair again, he turned her face to his. She watched him through wide, sexy brown eyes, her body trembling. He knew it was from arousal, not fear. He could smell the lust pouring off her and he needed to taste her. His gaze narrowed on her full, pouty lips as they parted, and she panted softly. Her tongue snuck out to nervously moisten them and he lost it. Capturing her mouth roughly with his, Ryker groaned loudly at the sweet taste of her. Josie whimpered as he tightened his hold on her hair and slipped his tongue past her lips. Tasting her over and over again, he moved his hips, pressing his throbbing cock up into the softness of her bottom. God, he wanted her. He wanted to take her right there, shoving into her wet heat. He wanted to sink his fangs deep into her skin, claiming her as his. Groaning, Ryker pulled away from Josie. Breathing harshly, he fought to get himself back under control. He was not claiming his mate in a fucking hospital.

When he finally felt like he could talk, he rasped, "I need to get you home, Sweetheart. I want to get you into a nice, hot bubble bath. I need to take care of you and make sure you are settled in and safe before I have to leave." When Ryker mentioned his intent to leave, Josie seemed to close down. Drawing back away from him, she attempted to rise, but he pulled her back. Resting his forehead against hers, he whispered, "I don't want to leave you, Josie. I really don't. But there is a fox shifter out there that needs me right now. Her name is Chloe Samson and she was stolen from her home by some rogue wolf shifters. If I don't go find her, she will end up dead, if she isn't already."

Gasping, Josie hurriedly stood up, and grabbing his hand, pulled him to his feet. Her eyes wide with fear, she pushed Ryker toward the door. "Go, Ryker! Go with Storm now," she insisted. "I will be fine. I can have Slade and Charlotte meet me here and take me home. You have to help Chloe."

His Josie had a heart of gold. Ryker could see it, could feel it. He was so proud to call her his. Gathering her into his arms again, he pressed a brief kiss on her lips. "I will go after you are settled in your bath, Josie. Not before. I need to make sure you are taken care of before I leave. Storm is making some calls now and we will have to wait to hear back from our contacts, so we have time." Removing his coat, he wrapped it around her slight frame. "Do you have extra socks around here?" he asked, glancing at her small feet.

"Yes, in my office." Lacing her fingers with his, Josie led him down the hall to her office where she pulled a pair of warm, fuzzy Christmas socks out of her drawer. Drawing them on her feet, she went to a closet and grabbed the extra pair of tennis shoes she kept there. After putting them on and lacing them, she stood and once again slipped her fingers into Ryker's. "I'm ready," she said with a soft, shy smile.

After assuring the nurses several times that Josie was fine, they left the hospital and made their way to Josie's house.

"Most of the pack live in apartments, but I wanted a home. A place to call my own. My house is on the outskirts of our small town. It backs up to the forest, and I have a balcony off my bedroom where I can sit and enjoy the peace and quiet," she told Ryker on the way. "I love it." Pausing, she looked up at him in concern. "What do we do now, Ryker? This is my home. I have lived here for over thirty years and this pack is my family. I don't want to leave, but you have a job with the council. You won't be able to stay here. I'm sure they require you to be wherever they are to protect them when you aren't out hunting down rogue wolves."

Cupping her cheek in his hand, Ryker leaned down and softly kissed her lips. "Let's not worry about that right now. Right now I just want to get you home and take care of you. We can worry about all of this when my mission is over, and I know you are safe."

Nuzzling his hand, she whispered, "Okay. We need to get to know one another, too, Ryker. I don't know anything about you, except that you are an enforcer for the council and your body is pure sin." Blushing at the words that had slipped out, Josie quickly hid her face in his chest.

Chuckling, Ryker lifted her chin up and kissed her softly one more time. "I'm glad you approve." Still laughing, he continued to Josie's house, mulling over the different possibilities for their future. He wanted to make Josie happy, but he had obligations, too. There had to be a way to make it work. He was not giving Josie up, but he needed her to be happy with any decisions they made.

When they reached Josie's house, Ryker paused by the front door and took out his Glock. Looking at him quizzically, Josie whispered, "There isn't anyone here, Ryker. I'm safe in the compound."

"Humor me," he muttered. Finding the door unlocked, he scowled at her and held up a finger for silence when she would have defended herself. He did not care if she lived in the White River compound and considered the whole pack her family, she was his and he took care of his own. From now on, that door would be locked when Josie was not home. Hell, it would be locked when she was home.

Silently, they entered the small house. It did not take long to check the living room, kitchen, bathroom, and office that made up the downstairs. Making sure Josie stayed behind him, Ryker made his way upstairs. The two large bedrooms and bathroom were clear. Putting his gun away, he turned back to Josie. "Do not ever leave the door unlocked again when you are gone, Josie." Before she could interrupt, he pushed on, "And for now, keep it locked when you are home alone. You saw what happened with Hunter tonight. There is no way he was that far out just wandering around and got caught. Phoenix would never let him get that far away without supervision. Not only that, but he was in human form, not cub. Hunter is in his cub form seventy-five percent of the time. That man was here, Josie. Here in this town. And you said he knew Hunter was a shifter. You may have gotten this one, but there are others like him out there, and they will be back. I need to know that you are safe when I can't be here to protect you."

As he let everything he said sink in, Ryker moved to the bathroom and started the shower. Josie needed to get all of the blood washed off her body before she relaxed in the bath. There was a large claw foot tub in the corner. Since there was a shower, this tub was purely for his mate's pleasure. Ryker groaned at the thought of Josie in it, naked, bubbles up to her neck. Feeling his fangs once again fill his mouth, he shuddered and palmed his hard cock. Hell, he would give anything to get in that tub with her right now. He wanted to run his hands over her wet, silky skin. "Fuck", he growled softly.

Shaking off his thoughts, Ryker entered Josie's bedroom and found her out on the balcony. Stopping at the sliding glass doors, he leaned up against the doorjamb and watched her, soaking in her presence. She was standing with her back to him, her hands braced against the wrought iron. He could sense Josie's pain and wished he did not have to leave her. He had a feeling he was going to be gone hunting down the rogue wolves for at least a week, if not more. But when he was done, after he had checked in with the council, Ryker was coming back here. Back to his beautiful Doc Josie.

Stepping away from the doorway, Ryker moved up behind Josie. Slipping his arms around her waist, he settled her back against his hard body. Sighing, Josie leaned her head on him. She was so tiny that the top of her head just reached the middle of his chest. Nuzzling her cheek, he gently kissed the top of her ear, then slowly nipped and licked his way down to her bare shoulder where the too-big scrub top had fallen down. A soft moan escaped Josie's lips as she slid her arm up and cupped the back of his head, holding him against her.

"Josie," he whispered as he scraped the soft skin with his teeth. Josie's hold tightened and she pressed him closer. Her body trembled as she pushed back against him. Fighting for control, Ryker turned Josie around in his arms. He wanted to take her, to claim her right there, but there was not enough time to love and cherish her body like she deserved.

"Let's get you in the shower, Baby," he whispered. Bending down, he slipped an arm under her knees and swept her up into his arms. Taking her back into the house, he made his way to the bathroom.

Putting Josie on her feet, Ryker checked the water to make sure it was not too warm. Pulling her closer to the shower, he let go of her hand, and taking hold of her top, he gently slipped it up and over her head. Watching her carefully, he knelt down in front of her. Sliding his fingers into the waistband of her pants, he slid them slowly down, baring tantalizing skin on the way. Before he went too far, he stood up and backed away. "Take a quick shower, Josie. Then you can relax in a long, hot bubble bath."

While he waited for her to shower, Ryker went back into the bedroom to shut and lock the balcony doors. Turning down the covers on the bed, he closed his eyes and imagined loving his mate on it. Groaning, he reached down and adjusted himself. Breathing roughly, he raked a hand through his hair and fought for control.

Hearing the shower stop, Ryker went back to the bathroom and started the bath water. Turning, he walked over to the bathroom closet and found the bubble bath. After adding it to the water, he put the bottle back and waited for Josie to get out of the shower. He was going to put her in that tub and leave, even if it killed him. The way he was feeling, he would have blue balls for the next week.

"Fuck," he growled when she stepped out, drops of water sliding seductively down her skin. She was so damn sexy. He had to touch her. Going back to the tub, Ryker reached down and shut the water off. Turning back to

Josie, he held out his hand and waited until she stepped to him and tentatively placed her hand in his.

Ryker leaned down and licked at a water droplet sliding slowly down her neck. Palming a breast, he licked a bead of water off the nipple. He kissed and licked his way down to her belly button, before dropping to his knees. Pausing, Ryker rested his head against Josie's soft stomach. Shaking, fighting to keep himself from claiming her, he ran his hands around her waist and down to cup her wet bottom. He needed to leave. He knew he should leave. But he could not go without a taste of his mate. Slowly, Ryker kissed his way further down Josie's belly. Once he reached his destination, he found her clit and licked. As Josie cried out, he licked again and again. He had never tasted anything like her. She was unbelievable, so fucking good, and she was his. Growling, he brought a hand around and slipped two fingers inside of her, finding her wet and ready. When Josie cried out again, Ryker increased the rhythm of his fingers and sucked harder on her clit. Her moans grew louder and her whole body trembled, then she screamed as she came.

When Josie screamed, Ryker lost control. Rising, he pulled her against him and roughly took her mouth with his. Cupping her breast, he growled as he yanked his mouth away, breathing harshly. Backing her up, Ryker grabbed Josie's thighs and picked her up, sitting her on the counter by the sink. He yanked her hips toward him, and her hot wet heat pressed against his jean-covered cock. Snarling, Ryker leaned down and captured one of her nipples in his mouth. Sucking hard, he pushed his rock-hard erection against her again and again. He needed inside her now.

Reaching between them, Josie undid the buckle on his belt. "Oh God," she moaned, as Ryker switched over to the other breast, sucking and nipping at the nipple. After undoing the button on his jeans, she slowly slid the zipper down, and then shoved them down. Kicking them off, he pushed up against her, his long, thick length strained against her hot, slick opening.

Leaning back, he demanded, "Look at me." Ryker stilled until Josie stopped moving and locked her eyes with his. "Tell me you want this," he growled. "Tell me you are ready for this. We don't know each other, Josie. We have never met before tonight. Tell me you are not going to regret this when I am gone." He prayed she would say yes, say that she wanted this as badly as he did, but he refused to take her without her verbal permission.

Josie leaned her head back against the mirror above the counter, panting loudly. Running a hand through his thick, dark curls, she whispered, "You are mine, Ryker. I am yours. Whether we claim each other tonight, next week, or next month, that isn't going to change. I want you now. I want you inside of me. I need you."

That was all Ryker needed to hear. Holding her firmly by the hips, he leaned down and captured her mouth with his. Biting her lip, he tilted her hips and pushed his hard, straining cock deep inside her. As he began to move, he growled, "Mine. Mine." Pulling out, he pushed into her again and again. He wanted this. He wanted to spill inside his mate, while biting her, bonding them together. Suddenly, Josie rose up, wrapping her arms around him and Ryker felt her teeth sink deep into his shoulder. Letting out a roar, he let himself go, slamming into her faster and harder. As he came,

Ryker bit into her shoulder, claiming her for the world to see.

When Ryker released Josie's shoulder, he raised his head and looked into her eyes. He could get lost in her amazing, deep brown eyes. Lifting a hand, he traced a finger down her temple, over her cheekbone, stopping on her kiss-swollen lips. "I don't want to leave you," he confessed, leaning forward to kiss her again.

A tear slipped down her cheek as she whispered, "I don't want you to leave."

Gathering her in his arms, Ryker took Josie over to the waiting bathtub and slowly lowered her into it. Turning the water back on, he grabbed a sponge that sat on the side of the tub. After pouring some bath soap on it, he gently rubbed the sponge over her skin. Starting with her arms, he moved down her breasts and over her stomach. Lifting each sexy, silky-smooth leg out of the water, he washed them both before moving on to her back. When he had touched every inch of her body with the sponge, Ryker urged her up out of the water and quickly dried her off. He had taken up too much time, and wanted to tuck her into bed before he left. Wrapping her in a dry towel, he lifted her up in his arms and made his way to her bedroom. Sitting Josie on the bed, he found her warm fleece pajamas in a drawer where she said they were and helped her into them.

Pulling back the covers, Ryker waited until Josie slid into bed, then he pulled the covers around her, tucking her in. "I have to go," he told her quietly. "I don't want to, but Storm should have news by now and we need to get on the road."

Nodding, Josie clasped one of his large hands in hers,

placing a kiss on his scarred knuckle. "Go," she urged with a smile. "Go find Chloe. Find her and get her back to her family. I will be here when you are done."

Leaning in for one last kiss, Ryker reluctantly let go of Josie's hand. Taking out his cell phone, he asked her for her number. Typing it in, he called her cell. Josie had left it downstairs on the counter, but the number would be there in the morning. Standing, Ryker double checked the balcony doors and made sure all of the windows were locked.

"Be safe," he heard Josie whisper as he left her bedroom. Going through every room in the house, Ryker checked the locks on all of the windows and doors. As he left through the front door, he caught Slade's scent. After making sure the door was locked, he found Slade, who promised to watch over Josie for him. Taking one last walk around his mate's house to make sure everything on the outside was secure, Ryker made his way back to his truck where Storm was waiting.

"Anything?" he asked, as he climbed in and started the engine. Putting the vehicle in gear and leaving the compound was more difficult than he had thought it would be, but he got it done. As Storm filled him in on possible leads, Ryker only half listened. His mind was on the beautiful brunette he left nestled in bed waiting for his return.

3

Chase Montgomery stood by the window in his office, hands clenched tightly into fists. Sighing heavily, he stepped forward and leaned an arm against the window, resting his forehead against the cool glass.

Angel was here...on his land. Growling lowly, he squeezed his eyes shut, breathing roughly. His mate was out there in the darkness, only a couple of miles away. She and her team were investigating the attempted kidnapping of Phoenix's son. Even though it happened on his land, Chase had passed the investigation to Angel. She was more than capable of handling it, but that was not the real reason he gave up control. Chase could not handle being around Angel right now. He was so close to the edge that if he were near her, if he caught her scent, there was no way he would be able to hold back.

The mating bite on his shoulder throbbed sending a shot of pure lust straight to his dick. His body was in a constant state of arousal since Angel decided to bite him, starting the mate bonding process. Angel was running from him, but she would not be able to stay away long. He would not allow it, and his wolf would not be able to handle the separation much longer.

ANGEL and her team canvased the area surrounding the body of the dead man they tracked down from Josie's directions. "Shit, remind me not to piss the doc off," Jaxson said, as he searched through the man's pockets looking for anything that would give them a clue as to who he was and what he was doing on White River land. The man was lying in a pool of blood, from bite marks and deep gashes caused by Josie's claws. "No ID," he remarked. "Nothing at all on him. There was nothing in his coat, either."

"I found his truck, boss," Nico yelled as he jogged back toward Angel. "It's bare. Not a damn thing in it except a steel cage in the back. Not even registration."

"No sign of anyone else out there, Angel," Rikki reported when she and Flame approached the group. "The man was definitely here by himself."

"He may have been here alone, but he was part of something bigger," Flame retorted. Her eyes flashed in anger. "He had to be. There is no way he did all of this on his own."

Hands on her hips, Angel's gaze swept across the acres of land around them. "I agree. He may have been able to infiltrate pack lands, but how did he find out about shifters in the first place? Something else is going on here. I believe the immediate danger has been taken care of, but there is a much bigger threat out there."

Taking one last look at the dead body lying at her feet, she ordered, "Nico, go tell Chase what we know, which isn't much. We will continue looking into this, but for now the danger has been neutralized. The rest of you are with me. We need to clean up this mess. It needs to look like nothing happened."

Breathing deeply, Angel shut out the pain and frustration she could feel coming from Chase not too far from her. Fighting the urge to use her gift of telepathy and merge with him, she pushed thoughts of Chase from her mind. Now was not the time to dwell on what could not be. She had to put her children above her own desires. Until she could make sure they were all free of the General, there could be no Chase and Angel.

4

When Josie woke up the next morning, her first thought was that something was missing. Frowning in confusion, she slid her hand over to the far side of the bed, instinctively searching for something. Then memories of the night before slammed into her full force; Hunter's kidnapping and her part in stopping the man, which ended up causing his death. Even though the idea of what she had done caused her emotional heartache, Josie could not bring herself to regret killing Hunter's kidnapper. The alternative would have been much worse.

Her eyes widened when she remembered what happened after she had taken Hunter to the hospital. After putting stitches in Hunter's leg, she met her mate, Ryker. Tall, gorgeous, powerful Ryker. He was a council enforcer, who was at this very moment tracking down a pack of rogue wolves.

Slowly reaching up, Josie touched the bite mark on her neck from Ryker. The one that would tell everyone they were mates. A smile spread across her face as she remembered how lovingly Ryker had taken care of her after they claimed each other. Not only did he bathe her, but he dried her off, clothed her in warm pajamas, and snuggled her into bed.

Remembering that Ryker programmed her number into his phone, Josie jumped out of bed and ran downstairs to see if he had contacted her yet. Pulling up the missed call from him, she assigned his name to it. Disappointment set in when there was no call or text from him. Laughing to herself when she realized she was acting like a giddy teenager, Josie ran back upstairs and took a quick shower. After drying off, she quickly fixed her hair in a messy bun, put on a trace of makeup, and dressed in a pair of jeans and a bright red, warm sweater. She needed to stop by and check on Hunter and Serenity. After that, she had an appointment at her office with Janie, a woman who had been held captive at one of the General's facilities. She was having a difficult time moving on, so Josie made sure to see her at least once a week.

Josie checked her phone again after making her way back downstairs. Still nothing. A glance at the clock showed it was already late morning. Telling herself Ryker was on a mission and probably could not call, she mentally kicked herself for acting like a young girl in love. After eating a small breakfast, Josie grabbed her keys and phone, and then left the house, making sure to lock the door behind her. Slade and Charlotte were waiting outside to escort her to Phoenix and Serenity's. The walk was short, but Josie enjoyed the cold, brisk air on the way.

"Congratulations, Doc," Slade said with a grin before

leaving Josie at Serenity's door to parole the area while Josie was visiting.

Lightly touching her mate mark, Josie smiled. Ringing the doorbell, she waited for someone to answer while her thoughts were once again consumed by Ryker. When the door opened, she pushed thoughts of him to the back of her mind and concentrated on the woman and child in front of her.

AFTER SPENDING half an hour with Serenity and Hunter, Josie went to the hospital with Slade and Charlotte shadowing her this time. If she didn't know they were there, she would have missed them; they were that good.

Smiling as she walked through the front doors, Josie greeted everyone with a cheery wave. After grabbing a cup of coffee, she went to her office to get ready for her appointment. Turning her phone off, she put it in her desk drawer. Her patient needed her undivided attention and Josie did not want any distractions. Waiting for a call from Ryker was definitely a distraction.

While she waited, she sipped her coffee and thought about her patient. Janie had been kicked out of her pack almost four years ago for being a latent wolf shifter. For some reason that Josie had not figured out yet, Janie was unable to shift into her wolf form. Josie could not imagine not being able to run through the forest on all fours. It was one of the most exhilarating experiences. But nothing Josie tried had helped Janie shift.

After being kicked out of her pack, Janie made it on her own for a year before the General's men captured her.

She was held by them for a full two years before being rescued by RARE. During that time, Janie was raped and beaten by four different men. She was eight months pregnant when RARE rescued her, and now had a healthy, vibrant seven-month-old daughter named Alayna. Josie was not sure Janie would have survived if it was not for Alayna. She gave Janie a reason to live.

Lost in thought, the phone on her desk rang twice before she picked it up. "Why aren't you answering your damn cell?" Ryker demanded. As the sound of his voice flowed over her, Josie's day finally felt right, but that did not mean she was going to let him speak to her that way.

"Why did you wait this long to call?" she shot back. She was fifty-four years old, dammit. While that may not be old in wolf years, it meant she had been an adult for several years and no one was going to treat her like a child. Ryker better learn that lesson now.

"I was investigating some information we received on the rouge wolf pack. Information that didn't pan out," he growled. "I was worried, Josie. I can't be there for you right now. I need to know you are okay."

Slowly letting go of her anger, Josie responded, "I'm sorry, Ryker. I'm fine. But you cannot speak to me like I'm a child. I am a grown woman. I love that you want to be here for me and protect me, but your choice of words and tone of voice need to change."

Ryker let out a frustrated sigh. "It's hard to be away from you, Josie. It's hard to concentrate on my job because I am worried about you. I need my full attention on tracking down this pack. Instead, it is on you. I am wondering if you are safe. Wondering if Slade and Charlotte are doing a good enough job guarding you. If there are any males around you that I need to kill."

Laughing softly, Josie told him, "There are definitely no other males you need to worry about. Look, Ryker, you need to concentrate on your job, and I need to concentrate on mine. I can't be the doctor I need to be for my patients when I am sitting around waiting to hear from you."

"I know," Ryker reluctantly agreed, swearing softly. "I need to go, Sweetheart. Storm just got a hit on the pack. I am going to go silent until this job is done. Call me if you need me, otherwise I will be there as soon as I can."

Fighting the tears that threatened, Josie told Ryker goodbye and hung up the phone. She knew it was for the best, but that did not make her feel any better.

"Do I need to come back at another time?" a voice asked hesitantly from the open doorway. Realizing Janie had shown up early, Josie straightened her spine and promised herself she would do what she did best. She would throw herself into her job and try to ignore the fact that she now had a mate who she would not be talking to for several days.

As pain filled her heart, Josie rose from her chair and gestured to Janie to take a seat on the couch. Smiling fully, Josie sat beside Janie and talked for the next two hours about Janie's daughter, Alayna, her roommate, Flame, and anything else Janie wanted to talk about. Not once did Janie mention her time in captivity, but Josie knew she would one day. And Josie would be there for her when that day came. Janie needed her, the White River Wolves needed her. Maybe, someday, Ryker would need her, too.

5

One week later, Ryker still was not any closer to finding the rogue wolf pack. Every lead he and Storm were fed turned out to be false. Right now, he sat in the back corner of a seedy bar, pretending to nurse a beer. The last lead they were given said the pack liked to come to this hole in the wall dive. Storm was playing pool, flirting outrageously with some obviously cracked-out humans. She was trying to get them to leak information, but Ryker was positive this was another dead end.

Pulling his cell phone out of his pocket to text the council a progress report, he brought up Josie's number instead. He had not talked to her in one full week, and it was killing him. She was his mate, the other half of his soul. They had completed the full mate bond ritual and once that happened, it was hard for mates to be apart for a couple of days, let alone an entire week.

Go to her, Storm's voice whispered in his mind. *I will finish up here, Ryker. Go to your mate. You are of no help to me. Not like this.*

Ryker and Storm had both been born with the ability to speak telepathically. While they chose to use the gift with each other, they kept their ability secret from others. Not even the council knew what they could do. Storm could see into the future at times as well, but telepathy was Ryker's only gift.

I can't, Storm. I won't leave you. There was no way he was leaving Storm here by herself. She was more than capable of taking care of these clowns, but if for some reason the pack they were hunting did show up, she would need his help.

You and I both know they aren't coming here tonight. Storm responded. *Just go. You know mates can't stay away from each other for long. I don't know why you didn't wait to fully mate until our mission was over.*

The pull was too strong, Ryker admitted. *I couldn't help it. You will see one of these days, Storm. You think you can fight it, but when your mate is standing there in front of you, you just lose control.*

Yeah, I doubt I will ever know the feeling, Ry, Storm said with a touch of sadness in her voice. *I have waited so long, that I think I am ready to give up.*

Glancing up at Storm in surprise, Ryker watched as she took a shot, sinking the eight ball into a side pocket. *Okay, we are done here,* she announced. *They don't have any useful information for us.* Blowing the men a kiss, she told them goodbye and casually sauntered out of the bar.

Leaving his beer on the table in front of him, Ryker stood up and followed. Outside, he walked the two blocks to where they left his truck, his thoughts tormented once again by Josie. Climbing inside where Storm waited, he started the truck and turned on the heater. It was freezing out and they were calling for more snow. It would definitely be a white Christmas.

When they reached the rundown hotel they were staying at, Storm turned to him and grasped his arm tightly. "Ryker, go to your mate. She is only half an hour away. Go. I promise I will wait for you to return before I follow up on any new leads."

Shaking his head, Ryker put the truck in park. He refused to leave Storm. He learned his lesson the hard way with his last partner. Although, at that time, Ryker was the one that was left. When his partner went to spend time with his flavor of the week, Ryker was jumped by the people they were hunting and nearly killed. He was not going to let that happen to Storm. "I am not leaving you alone, Storm. Not going to happen."

Storm shrugged. "Fine, then let's go. I can sleep at Nico and Jenna's for the night." When Ryker stared at her in surprise, she said, "Ryker, you are my partner and my only true friend. I would do just about anything for you. You need a night with Josie, and I need your head back in the game. Let's go so we can both be happy."

Deciding Storm was right, Ryker put the truck in gear and headed toward Boulder. As Storm placed a call to the council to let them know they had hit another dead end, Ryker's thoughts turned once again to Josie.

It had been a week since they had spoken, but he called Slade daily to check on her. There were no repercussions as of yet for the man's life she had taken. RARE found the body and it had been disposed of, along with the truck that was parked on the edge of the White River Wolves' border. As far as RARE could tell, the man had been watching the compound for weeks. He watched long enough to figure out who was patrolling the area and when shift change was. Chase had tightened up security after the General kidnapped Lily, but some of his guards did not think it was necessary. It had become habit for the guards on duty to leave a few minutes early, while the next ones arrived late. Their lack of responsibility allowed the man to sneak onto pack lands during their shift change. All four were suspended of duty until further notice.

Hunter admitted to spotting a deer, which caused him to wander further from home than normal while Phoenix was taking a shower and Serenity was napping. He was in his human form because he and Phoenix were going Christmas shopping for Serenity. RARE had not found any incriminating evidence on the man or in his truck, so they had no idea who he worked for or what his exact plans had been with Hunter. The consensus at this time was that he was working alone that night.

However, Chase was not willing to give up the protection detail on either Hunter or Josie just yet. He also stepped up security around the far borders of his land. Chase had a feeling something was going to happen. There might not have been anyone with the man that night, but he obviously planned on taking Hunter somewhere to sell him. Someone was selling shifters for money, and Chase was not going to sit around and wait for the next kidnapping attempt against his pack.

As they neared the entrance to the White River Wolves' compound, Ryker realized he probably should have called Josie to let her know he was coming. But it was too late now. Ryker parked his truck in front of the hospital. He was not sure if she was working, or if she was home. It was after midnight, but that did not mean anything to a doctor.

Grabbing his duffle bag out of the back of the truck, he headed to the hospital as Storm went to Nico's. Entering the hospital, Ryker nodded to the nurse at the front desk. "Is Doc Josie in?" he asked.

"She went home an hour ago," the nurse replied. "The poor woman was exhausted. She has been working way too much lately."

Thanking her, Ryker left the hospital and went to Josie's. Slade stepped away from the side of the house when he saw Ryker. "Josie got home just a little bit ago. I have no idea how she is still moving. She has been at the hospital nonstop since you left. I was surprised to see her here so early tonight. She has always worked long hours, but this is ridiculous."

Raking a hand through his hair, Ryker closed his eyes tiredly. His mate was in pain and was trying to drown it out with work. He knew what she was doing, because he was doing the same thing. He did not want this for her. Unfortunately, right now there was nothing he could do about it. He should not even be here tonight, but he could not stay away any longer. Taking a deep breath, he took the key Slade offered him and walked up the front steps.

6

Josie was so tired that she fell into a deep sleep the minute her head touched the pillow. After Ryker left the week before, she had quickly learned working herself into exhaustion was the only way she could sleep. As she slept, she dreamt of Ryker. In her dream, he slid into bed beside her, pulling her against his hot, naked flesh. Running his hand up her leg, he slid it over her hip and gently cupped her breast. Moaning, she pushed back against the warm body behind her, calling out for him.

"Ssshhh, Sweetheart," Ryker whispered. "I'm right here."

The dream felt so real. She wanted it to be real. She wanted Ryker there in bed with her, touching her, loving her.

Throwing her head back, Josie whimpered as Ryker pinched her nipple. "Oh, Ryker," she moaned. "Touch me. I need you to touch me." His hand slid from her breast down to the top of her pajama pants. Sliding his hand in and over her mound, he slipped a finger inside her as he flicked her clit with his thumb. Josie's eyes snapped open as pleasure flooded her body. When the scent of her mate engulfed her, tears slipped down her cheeks at the realization that Ryker was really there.

Whispering his name on a tortured moan, Josie arched back into him. Ryker lightly kissed her slender neck, from just below her ear down to where his mating bite showed. Slowly he pushed her pajamas down her smooth, milky white legs, removing them. Trailing a hand up the back of her leg, he slipped it under her knee, lifting it up to slide inside her.

"No," Josie protested softly. "I want to see you." Turning around, she pushed Ryker onto his back and straddled him. Drowning in his dark gaze, she grabbed the hem of her nightshirt and pulled it up over her head, throwing it to the side of the bed. Bringing her hands back down, she ran them over her breasts, moaning as they skimmed over her sensitive nipples.

"You are so sexy," Ryker rasped. Grabbing her hips tightly, he raised her up and lowered her onto his hot, hard length. She gasped as he started to move slowly. Sliding a hand down from her breast, she lightly touched her clit, groaning at the liquid fire running through her veins. With one hand working a nipple and one her clit, she rode Ryker, panting loudly.

"Fuck!" Ryker roared as he came. Rearing up, he sank his teeth into Josie's shoulder, claiming his mate again. Crying out, Josie sank her own teeth into Ryker's shoulder as she came.

They stayed like that for several minutes before Ryker lifted her off him and snuggled her into the covers beside him. Cradling her to his chest, he gently stroked her soft hair. Kissing her softly on the top of her head he whispered, "I have to leave in the morning. I shouldn't be here now, but I couldn't stay away from you any longer. We haven't been able to hunt down the wolf pack. Chloe is still out there. I have to track them down, Josie. I have to find them."

Leaning up on an elbow, Josie gazed down at him. Reaching out, she lightly traced the hard contours of his face. He was so handsome, so fierce. "You will find them, Ryker. I know you will," she said.

"None of our leads have panned out," Ryker told her. "The longer they have her, the more likely it is that she will not make it. I hate to think of what she is going through right now."

"You will find her, Ryker," Josie vowed. "I know you will. You will not stop until you do. Being apart from each other is hard, but helping people like Chloe is what you do. If you don't find her, if you don't save her, no one else will. You have to do this, Ryker, and you will. I know you will." Placing a kiss on his cheek, then on his lips, she whispered, "Thank you. Thank you for coming to me."

"I couldn't stay away. I needed to feel you next to me," Ryker admitted. Tenderly, he ran a hand down the side of her face. "I need to know more about you, Josie. I want to know your favorite color. Your favorite movie. What you like to do in your spare time. I want to know everything there is to know about you."

Smiling, she murmured, "I want that too, Ryker." Wrapped in each other's arms, they talked well into the night, sharing their lives with one another. Until finally, they fell asleep.

Ryker was gone when Josie woke up the next morning.

There was a dark red rose on the pillow next to her. Her heart filling with what could only be love, she picked up the rose. Running the petals over her face, feeling the softness against her skin, Josie smiled. He would be back, she knew, but right now, he had a job to do, and so did she.

7

Ryker prowled through the dark streets of Denver with new purpose. Thoughts of Josie were constantly on his mind. He was driven by his need to find the rogue wolf pack so he could move on with his life. He had some difficult decisions to make, and he was ready to deal with them. Leaving Josie two days ago had been one of the hardest things Ryker had ever been required to do. He had never felt for anyone the way he did Josie. Ryker was not a sweet, tender person. He was a hard, dominant male with an alpha personality. But when he was with Josie, all he wanted to do was care for her, cherish her, and show her how much she meant to him. He was a goner, and he knew it.

Ryker was going to find that wolf pack, he was going to save the young female fox shifter, and then he was going to go home to his mate. He and Storm had a new tip they were following, and he had a good feeling about it. He felt like they were finally on the right track.

"There's the warehouse," Ryker said in a low voice,

motioning to the building up ahead. They moved silently forward, making the decision to speak only telepathically now. They were too close to their prey and did not want to give up the element of surprise. Slowly they canvased the building, making a wide trip around the outside. Stopping suddenly, Storm held up a hand. *Talk to me, Storm,* Ryker ordered. He trusted Storm. If she sensed something, something was there.

They are here, she said, looking over at him with an excited gleam in her eye. *We finally found them, Ryker. They are fucking here. I can smell them. They are rank as hell. I can smell the fox. She is still alive, and she is terrified.*

Giving a short nod, Ryker ordered, *You take the south side. I'll take the north.*

Silently, Storm merged into the shadows surrounding the building. Ryker moved to the north side of the building and slipped through a broken window on the ground floor. They needed to move fast. They had to find Chloe before the pack scented them.

Palming his Glock, Ryker moved swiftly down the empty hallway. Hearing a faint noise above him, he found the stairs and stealthily made his way to the second floor. *I hear something, Storm. Second floor.*

Already on it, she replied. *I'm on my way up now.* Slowly inching the door open at the top of the stairs, Ryker peered around the corner. Nothing. Slipping through the door, he quietly shut it behind him. Ryker paused and listened intently. The noise was coming from the left. *East side of the building,* he told Storm.

On it, was her quick response.

Halfway down the deserted hallway, Ryker found what he was looking for. Seeing Storm moving toward him, he held up one finger and then pointed to the door. Glancing through a window on the door, he saw a large, open room with no furniture. Huddled in a corner was a small woman with long auburn hair curled up into a ball. Her clothes were torn and dirty, and there were dark bruises on her skin that was exposed.

There were three men and one woman in the room with her. The stench was horrible. It was no wonder the wolves didn't scent Ryker and Storm. As if sensing Ryker's eyes on her, the young woman raised her head. Looking fearfully around the room, she froze when her gaze landed on him. He shook his head once, holding a finger to his lips. Eyes widening in hope and understanding, the woman tucked her head into her knees, turning her face to the wall.

Let's do this, Storm growled fiercely. Sliding a knife out of the holster on her leg, she waited impatiently.

With one last look at Storm, Ryker opened the door. The rogue female wolf saw them first. Screeching loudly, she pulled a knife out of her jeans and raised her arm, aiming in their direction. Ryker lifted his Glock and pulled the trigger, putting a silver bullet between her eyes. With a quick glance to his right, Ryker saw Storm's knife leave her hand. It hit the intended target, impaling itself into the neck of one of the men. Her gun went off immediately afterward, putting a silver bullet directly into the heart of another one.

The last wolf quickly shifted and came after Ryker. Before he could lift his gun, the wolf had his jaws wrapped tightly around Ryker's wrist. Snarling when he felt sharp teeth sink into his skin, Ryker slammed his fist into the wolf's head. The minute he let go, Ryker shot him. Watching the wolf writhe in pain as it slowly died, Ryker growled, "Silver bullets, asshole. You won't be getting back up." Ryker had learned over a century ago, there were only three ways to kill a shifter and make absolutely sure it was dead. A knife to the heart, silver bullets, or decapitation. Ryker preferred bullets because they made less of a mess.

Hearing quiet sobs, Ryker swiftly made his way over to the female still huddled in the corner. "It's going to be all right, Chloe," he told her gently. "I'm Ryker, and this is Storm. We were sent by the Shifter Council to find you and return you to your family."

"No!" the woman screamed. "No! You cannot take me back there. They are the reason I am here."

Looking at her in confusion, Storm said, "But, they are the ones that contacted the council and told them you were missing. They said that a wolf pack had kidnapped you and asked the council to find you."

"No," the woman shook her head adamantly. "They sold me to the wolf pack. They paid them to take me away from home. They wanted to get rid of me. I don't know why they went to the council, unless they thought I would be dead by now, but they are the reason I am here. You cannot take me back there. I won't go!"

Ryker and Storm's eyes locked in uncertainty. Their orders were to retrieve Chloe Samson and deliver her directly to her family, but there was obviously more to the story than what the council had been told. Until they knew the truth, Ryker was not handing Chloe over to anyone.

"Come with us, little fox," he said softly, reaching out a hand to her. "Come on. My mate lives nearby. She is a doctor and will take care of you while Storm and I figure this out."

"You won't take me back to my family?" Chloe asked, her amber eyes bright with fear. "I can't go back there. I won't."

"No, we won't take you to your family," Ryker promised. Staring at Ryker's large hand in terror, Chloe shook as tears escaped her eyes. "Come on, little fox," Ryker tried again. Smiling encouragingly, he coaxed, "Josie will take care of you when we get to her hospital. I promise. We need to get those wounds looked at."

Swallowing hard, Chloe lowered her head to look at the bruises on her body. There was blood on her back seeping through her shirt where she had been clawed, and a long rip in her jeans where blood trickled down. "Roxy, the female wolf, didn't like it when the males looked at me. She wanted them all to herself." Shrugging, Chloe whispered, "I didn't mind her beating me. At least the males left me alone because of her."

Ryker sighed in relief. He was glad the young woman had not been sexually assaulted. It was going to be hard enough to move on from this terrifying experience as it was.

Ryker waited patiently for Chloe to decide whether or not he could be trusted. Finally, she reached out and placed her hand hesitantly in Ryker's. 'I can't shift," she admitted. "My fox is scared. She is hiding from me. No matter how hard I try, I can't get her to show herself." If Chloe were able to shift, she would heal much faster, but that wasn't going to happen right now.

Helping Chloe to her feet, Ryker scanned her quickly to assess her physical state. Several claw marks and bruises, but no broken bones. She was shaky and could not stand on her own at first, but that was to be expected. Not only was she scared, but he wondered how long she had been on the floor curled into a ball, trying not to attract any attention.

As he helped her stand, her eyes suddenly widened in fear and she screamed out a warning. Swinging around, Ryker watched in shock as Storm's eyes widened in stunned surprise and a painful gasp escaped her lips. Slowly, her knees buckled and she slid to the floor, the hilt of a knife protruding from her back. Behind her, Ryker saw a man they had missed. Throwing his head back, the bastard let out a maniacal laugh. "Got your bitch, didn't I?" he bragged loudly. Laughing again, the man pulled a gun out of the back of his pants. "Now it's your turn."

Letting out a loud roar, Ryker let his beast free. Shifting quickly into his bear, he was on the man before he could utter a sound, tearing him apart piece by piece. The bastard deserved to die a horrible death after what he did to Storm. Ryker and Storm had been partners for over thirty years. She was tough, sassy, funny, and very loyal. She was his best friend. And she was lying on the floor, bleeding out.

Getting a tight grip on his anger, Ryker backed away from what was left of the man who had hurt Storm. Shifting, ignoring his state of undress, Ryker hurried to where she lay on the hard concrete floor. Kneeling beside her, he gently brushed her hair away from her face.

Panting softly, Storm whispered, "I fucked up, Ry."

Ryker cursed when he realized he could not pull the knife out. The long blade was embedded into Storm's back on the same side as her heart. He was not sure how close it was, and he was not willing to take any chances.

"You did just fine, Storm," Ryker told her gruffly. Glancing up at Chloe, he said, "We need to get out of here now. Can you walk?"

"Yes," Chloe sniffled, barely holding in her own tears. "Yes, I can walk. Let's go." Heading for the door on wobbly legs, she stopped and turned to look back at him. "You need clothes."

Cursing, Ryker realized he could not go running through the streets with his dick hanging out.

"Wait," Chloe said, rushing from the room as quickly as she could on her shaky legs. Five minutes later she was back with a black duffle bag in her hands. "None of the men that took me were as big as you, but maybe you can wear something in here," she said, shoving the bag toward him.

Grabbing the bag, Ryker rummaged through it and found a pair of jogging pants and a tee shirt. They were smaller than his normal size, but he didn't give a shit. All he cared about was getting Storm to a doctor. After quickly dressing, Ryker put on his boots that had somehow made it through his shift, and then knelt back down next to Storm. She was watching him through pain-filled tears. "I'm going to have to move you, Storm," he told her as he slipped his arms under her body. "This is going to hurt like a bitch, but I don't have a choice."

Slowly, Ryker lifted Storm in his arms, cradling her to his chest, careful of the knife still sticking out of her back. "I can't pull the knife out, Storm. I don't know how near your heart is. You might bleed out before I can get you to the hospital."

"Just let me go," Storm moaned in pain. "Please, Ryker, just let me go."

"No way in hell." Ryker growled, as he moved swiftly out the door and to the stairs. Waiting for Chloe to push the door open, he demanded, "Push through the fucking pain, Storm. You push through it, you hear me? I refuse to let you go, dammit!"

Storm's hand curled tightly into his borrowed shirt and she cried out in pain as Ryker took the stairs, two at a time. Once they cleared the front door of the building, Ryker sprinted the six blocks to his truck, Chloe on his heels. Chloe opened the back door of the extended-cab and Ryker gently laid Storm on the seat. "I'm taking you to Josie, Storm. You hold on, you hear me?" he shouted. "You do not leave me!"

Chloe climbed up into the back to sit with Storm, softly stroking her hair and murmuring gentle words of encouragement, while Ryker jumped into the front seat. Reaching under the dash, he grabbed the key where he had hidden it. Starting the truck, he threw it in gear and headed out of the city. Once he made it to the highway, he found his cell phone attached to the top of the visor and punched in Josie's number. When he heard her voice on the other end of the line, he struggled for control. "I need you, Josie," he whispered though his pain. "I need you. Storm is hurt. I...I don't know if she is going to make it. She's my partner, Josie. My best friend. My family."

"Talk to me, Ryker," Josie ordered briskly, "What happened? Where are you?"

Gripping the phone tightly, Ryker told her how the last man caught them off guard and was able to sink a knife deep into Storm's back near her heart. "I'm on my way. I should be there in twenty minutes," he said when he saw the sign for Boulder.

"Get Storm here, Ryker. I will get the operating room ready. You get her here, and I will save her," Josie vowed.

Swallowing hard, Ryker tightened his hold on the steering wheel. He could hear Josie shouting orders to the nurses, but he could not understand what she was saying. "Baby," he whispered. He needed to hear her voice.

"I'm here," she said, "but I have to go. I need to get everything ready. I will save her, Ryker," she promised. "Your job is to get her here; I will take care of the rest."

After disconnecting the call, Ryker placed a call to Charlene with the shifter council. Reporting in, he relayed what happened and that he was on his way to the shifter hospital run by the White River Wolves. After confirming that he did have Chloe Samson with him, and quickly explaining why she could not be immediately returned to her family, he ended the call.

Gripping the steering wheel tightly, Ryker pressed down on the gas pedal. Charlene would order a cleanup crew to dispose of the mess he had left behind. Right now, Ryker's main concern was Storm.

Ten minutes later, he pulled through the gates of the compound without stopping to check in. When Ryker cleared the doorway of the hospital, Josie was ready for him.

After gently placing Storm down on her stomach on the gurney the nurses had waiting, Ryker knelt down beside her. "You are going to be just fine, Storm," he promised, looking into her tear-filled, silver gaze. "Josie is going to take care of you."

Closing her eyes, Storm whispered, "I don't know if she can, Ryker. I think it might be too bad this time."

"Why don't you let me be the judge of that," Josie said, as she stepped forward and knelt beside Ryker. Clasping one of Storm's hands in hers, Josie told her, "I am going to fix this, Storm. I am a doctor. This is what I do. Trust me."

A tear escaped as Storm whispered, "If Ryker trusts you, I trust you." Leaning forward, Ryker gently nuzzled Storm's cheek with his own, giving her the comfort she needed. Allowing her eyes to close, Storm demanded in a low voice, "Take care of Chloe."

Nodding, Ryker stood up and backed away, watching as the nurses wheeled Storm down to the end of the hall, Josie holding her hand the whole way.

After they entered a door that said 'Surgery' above it, Ryker turned his attention to the nervous fox shifter behind him. "Come on," he said gruffly. "They will be in there awhile. We need to go meet with the alpha, Chase Montgomery. He needs to know what happened and that you are here." When Chloe flinched, Ryker promised, "You will be fine. You are on White River land. Chase will protect you while you are here. And until we get to the bottom of who sold you to the wolf pack and why, you are under my protection. No one will harm you."

As Chloe reluctantly followed Ryker to Chase's office in another building, Ryker had to make himself focus on the task at hand. He was worried about Storm, but knew Josie would do everything she could to save her.

Reaching the closed door to Chase's office, Ryker knocked and waited for permission to enter. Hearing Chase's muffled response to come in, Ryker opened the door and stepped back, allowing Chloe to enter first.

Timidly, she stepped through the doorway, stopping just over the threshold.

Chase sat behind his large, cherry colored wood desk. He was staring intently at the computer, but shifted his attention to them after a moment. Standing, he came around his desk, and raising his eyebrows at Ryker's attire said, "I have some clothes in the closet in the bathroom that should fit you. Go change. You reek."

Baring his teeth at the insult, Ryker ignored him. Placing a hand gently on Chloe's shoulder, Ryker introduced her to Chase. "Chloe is the fox shifter that Storm and I were sent by the council to track down. Supposedly, Chloe's family is worried about her and wants her back, but according to Chloe, her family is responsible for her being taken in the first place. They paid the pack to kidnap her and take her far away from home."

Eyes narrowing, Chase growled, "Why would they do that? And then why go to the council to get her back?"

"We never had the chance to discuss why." Turning to her, Ryker asked, "Do you know why they would want to have you kidnapped, Chloe?"

The fear evident on her face, Chloe whispered, "My step dad, Gentry Samson, is the one who sold me. He has never wanted me around. My mom married him fifteen years ago when I was nine. At first, he was wonderful. He wined and dined her, treated me like I was his own daughter. After they got married, things changed. He started beating us daily, keeping food from us so that we stayed weak, and locking us in our home away from others. We were both too scared to try and run. I would have found a way to leave when I turned eighteen, but I couldn't leave my mom. She never would have survived living there without me, but there was no way Gentry would let her go."

"Are they fated mates?" Chase asked curiously.

"No," Chloe told him, shaking her head. "My mom has never met her fated mate. She became pregnant with me when she was seventeen by a boy she thought loved her. Once he heard she was pregnant, he ran. We were barely scraping by when she met Gentry. I think that is part of the reason he held so much appeal. At the time, he offered a roof over our heads, and food on our plates."

"Why didn't you go to your alpha?" Chase asked. "As your alpha, it is his job to take care of both you and your mother. If your mother and Gentry aren't fated mates, he should have stepped in and removed you from the home."

Chloe looked at her feet for a moment. Taking a deep breath, she raised her head, her eyes connecting with Chase's. "Gentry is the alpha," she explained. "We don't live in a large pack like wolves. There is only Gentry, Mom and I, and two other families. There was no one else to turn to. Gentry is too strong. No one will challenge him. They are too afraid."

"Where are you from?" Chase questioned.

"Near Alexandria, Minnesota. We live about five miles south of town," Chloe replied. "There are three houses, all in Gentry's name. As alpha, he controls all of the money and assets."

"I still don't understand why Gentry would have bothered going to the council to ask them to track you down. It doesn't make sense. Then he would be caught in his own lie," Ryker said.

"The pack was supposed to kidnap me, take me a couple of states away, and kill me. That's why Gentry had you look for me. He thought I was dead. Gentry took out a life insurance policy on both myself and my mother a few years ago. I guess he thought it was time to cash it in." Her jaw clenched tightly, Chloe said, "I can't go back. I won't. But I need to find a way to get my mother out of there. When Gentry finds out I am alive, he might kill her."

Leaning back against his desk, Chase crossed his arms over his wide chest. Narrowing his eyes, he asked, "Do you want to be a part of my pack, Chloe?"

Her eyes widened, "But I'm not a wolf. I'm a fox."

"It doesn't matter," Chase told her gently. "I don't discriminate in my pack. I will give you a place to live, protection, food, and I will help you find a job. You will have nothing to fear in my pack, Chloe. No one here will hurt you."

Her eyes alight with hope, Chloe asked, "What about my mother? I can't leave her there alone."

"You let me worry about your mother," Chase said. "I'm your alpha now. It's my job to take care of you. That includes helping your mother."

Wrapping her arms tightly around herself, tears flowing unchecked down her cheeks, Chloe whispered, "Thank you, Alpha. Thank you so much."

Pushing away from his desk, Chase closed the distance between them. Settling a hand gently on her shoulder, he let some of his power flow from himself to her, slowly easing the tension in her body and calming her. "You need to go get some food and rest, Chloe. I have some phone calls to make."

"I can't rest right now," Chloe whispered. "We need to get back to the hospital. We have to check on Storm."

"Storm? What happened to Storm?" Chase growled.

Ryker filled him in on the situation, starting with the tip that was called in and ending with Storm being taken to surgery. "Tell me you got them all," Chase demanded.

"Yes," Ryker nodded, a dangerous glint in his eyes. "They are all dead."

"Good." Chase pointed toward his bathroom, "You really need to put on different clothes before you go anywhere."

With a snarl, Ryker entered the bathroom and quickly changed. When he was finished, he threw the offensive clothes in the trash before heading back to the hospital with Chloe.

SITTING AT HIS DESK, Chase contemplated the situation, trying to decide his best course of action. There was no way he was going to allow Chloe to go back to her stepfather, and he needed to get her mother away from Gentry, too. If there was one thing Chase could not stand, it was the abuse of women and children. He would not willingly stand by and allow the abuse to continue. He could handle the situation himself, but he had another idea.

Taking out his cell phone, Chase found the number he needed. One he had only called a handful of times. Closing his eyes, he raked a hand through his thick, dark black hair. His hand tightened on the arm of his chair when he heard Angel's voice. "I have a job for you," he told her.

"What do you need?" she inquired. Chase could hear the faint sound of the television in the background before

Angel shut it off. He closed his eyes, picturing her in bed resting against the headboard. Silently telling himself to get a grip, he began. "Ryker and Storm were sent to Denver to track down a female fox shifter who was kidnapped. They rescued her tonight, but it seems the story that was told to the council was a lie. The woman's stepfather actually sold her to a pack of rogue wolves with the intention of having her taken and killed so he could collect some insurance money. Chloe, the fox, told us her stepfather has been abusing both Chloe and her mother for years. He is not her mother's fated mate, which means he has no permanent ties to her. I need you to go in and get Chloe's mother out of there before he kills her. Chloe is now a part of my pack. She is under my protection. Her mother will be, too." Standing up and walking over to the window, Chase peered out into the darkness. "Also, Storm was hurt tonight. She is in the hospital in critical condition. We don't know if she is going to make it."

"Shit," Angel swore. "Text me the details on Chloe and her mother. We will leave right away. Take care of Storm, Chase. I will come to the hospital as soon as I can."

"Josie has her in surgery right now. I am going over there as soon as I talk to the council." Lightly resting a hand on the cool glass in front of him, Chase said, "I will pay whatever your normal fee is for an extraction."

There was complete silence on the other end of the line, then Angel growled, "The hell you will," before hanging up. Sliding the phone back into his pocket, Chase groaned. Once again, he had somehow managed to piss his mate off.

8

J osie stripped off her latex gloves, throwing them into the trashcan by the door. She was exhausted. The surgery lasted five hours, and she'd almost lost Storm twice, but Josie refused to let her go. She heard the fear and pain in Ryker's voice earlier and knew Storm was important to him. She was not going to allow her to die. Storm had a long road to recovery ahead of her, but she would make it.

Josie pushed open the door and made her way to the waiting room where she found Ryker and Chloe. Chloe was curled up on a chair in the corner, her long hair covering her face. Dark bruises covered every exposed piece of skin Josie could see. The woman had obviously been to hell and back.

Walking over to where Ryker stood gazing out the window on the far wall, Josie slipped an arm around his waist, leaning into his side. They stood like that for several minutes watching the sunrise.

"She's going to make it," Josie told him, burrowing closer into his side. "It was touch and go for a while, but she's a fighter, Ryker."

"She wanted to give up," Ryker whispered in a tormented voice. "She begged me to leave her there to die. She is lonely, Josie. I'm all that she has."

"We aren't going to let her give up," Josie promised. "I will be with her every day, Ryker. Together, we will help her get through this."

Turning her to face him, Ryker slipped his fingers in her hair and pulled her close for a soft kiss. "Thank you, Josie. Thank you for everything." Resting his forehead on hers, he said, "I have to go meet with the council. They want me to give them a full report. I need to leave now."

Reaching up, Josie trailed her fingers across his strong jawline. "I understand. I will take care of Storm while you are gone."

"And Chloe," Ryker said. "Chloe needs you, too."

"Chloe?" Josie asked in confusion. "Isn't she going back to her family?"

"No. She needs to stay here with you, Josie. She needs your help. Her stepfather has abused Chloe and her mother for years. There is no way in hell she is going back there. Chase is working on freeing her mother now. He has offered them both a place in the pack."

"I will take care of her, Ryker," Josie told him. Raising her hand, she slid her fingers through his soft curls. "She can stay with me. I have room."

Kissing her gently on the top of the head, Ryker vowed, "I will be back. I don't know when, but I promise you, I will be back as soon as I can."

"I will be waiting," Josie whispered, as she pulled him down for another kiss. "I will always wait for you."

Rubbing his cheek against hers, Ryker chuffed softly. Squeezing her tightly to him, he whispered, "I love you, Mate."

Josie felt a tremor flow through her body at Ryker's words. He loved her. He was coming back, and he loved her.

Leaning back, Josie palmed his cheek. "I love you, too," she whispered. "Hurry home, Ryker."

With one last kiss, Ryker left the room. Josie watched out the window as he strolled to his truck. Opening the driver side door, he paused. Looking back at the hospital, his eyes searched the windows until he found Josie. Raising his hand, he smiled before sliding in behind the wheel and shutting the door.

Josie watched with a heavy heart as Ryker left the compound. It was hard to watch him go, even knowing he would be back. Sighing deeply, she made herself turn away from the window and walk over to Chloe. Kneeling down beside her, Josie gently touched her shoulder. Jumping in fear, Chloe sprang off the chair and rushed to the opposite side of the room. Falling to her knees, Chloe crawled the last few steps and huddled in a corner. She wrapped her arms tightly around her legs, and buried her head in her knees, her sobs loud and full of pain. For the first time, Josie caught sight of the dried blood that had soaked through the back of Chloe's ripped shirt.

"Chloe, it's just me," Josie reassured her quickly, standing up and holding her hands out to her sides in a nonthreatening way. "It is okay, Chloe. I'm Doc Josie, remember? You are at the hospital. You came in last night with Ryker and Storm." Moving slowly across the room, Josie stopped a few feet from her. "You are safe, Chloe. No one is going to hurt you here. I promise."

Moving closer, Josie settled on the floor beside Chloe. Crooning to her softly, Josie reached out and gently stroked her hair. "You are okay, Chloe. You are at the hospital with me and you are safe."

Hesitantly raising her head, Chloe looked at Josie through bright amber eyes. "I will never be safe as long as Gentry Samson is alive. Never."

Tucking a strand of stunning auburn hair behind Chloe's ear, Josie smiled gently. "You are part of our pack now, Chloe. We will all keep you safe. You do not have to worry about your stepfather anymore." Opening her arms, she tugged Chloe into them, careful of the wounds on her back. Rocking slowly, Josie held Chloe for several minutes. When she was sure Chloe was ready, she coaxed, "Let's get you looked at, Chloe. I want to clean your wounds and then I need to check on Storm. Afterwards, I would like you to come home with me so we can both get some rest. I have an extra room you can use until your mom arrives."

"Your alpha is really going to free my Mom?" Chloe asked, obviously afraid to hope. "He is going to bring her here?"

"*Our* alpha is going to bring your mom home, Chloe," Josie corrected. "He is your alpha now, too. You can trust him."

Swallowing hard, Chloe nodded. "Okay. I will try."

"That's all I can ask," Josie responded. "You will see over time that he can be trusted and that you are safe."

Rising, Josie held out a hand to Chloe. "Come on, let me bandage your wounds. Then I will check on Storm and we will get out of here." After a few moments, Chloe placed her hand in Josie's. It was a start, Josie thought with a smile. It was a start.

9

U nder the cover of darkness, RARE stealthily canvased the area inhabited by Gentry Samson's small pack. Jaxson had easily found the three houses titled in Gentry's name that Chloe had mentioned to Chase. All were in very poor condition; nothing but small, rundown shacks. Leaving the families asleep in the first two houses, RARE surrounded the last one. *Two people inside, boss,* Nico relayed. *A woman sitting on the floor in the corner of the bedroom. A man passed out in the living room.* Everyone on the team had the ability to speak telepathically. It was one of Angel's requirements to be a part of the team, one that could make the difference between life or death on a mission.

I'm in position, Rikki told them. She had found a tree to hide out in and her sniper rifle was trained on the man who sat in a chair in the living room, a beer can resting against his ample stomach.

That fucker moves, you take him out, Angel ordered. She was not messing around with Chloe's mother's life.

Got it, Rikki responded.

Jaxson and Nico, keep an eye on the other houses. Flame, you are with me. Flame followed Angel as she slipped silently around to the north side of the house. Angel tested the bedroom window first. Finding it nailed shut from the outside, she moved on to the next window. Swearing softly when she realized they were all nailed shut she growled, *Change of plans. The bastard has nailed all of the windows shut. There is no way we are getting in through one without waking him up. That woman has been traumatized enough. I don't want her to watch her husband die, no matter how much of a jackass he is. It will just cause more nightmares. We are going to try going through the front door. Nico, I need you with us.*

Meeting Nico at the front of the house, Flame and Angel waited while he reached out and turned the door-knob, quietly pushing the door open. The only sound that could be heard was the loud snoring from the man in front of the fire. Shutting the door behind them, they silently moved through the house to the bedroom. The woman gasped, crying out softly in fear when Nico opened the bedroom door. She cowered in the corner, her arms covering her head.

Flame quickly moved to her, kneeling down and gently running a hand over her hair, whispering, "Shhh, it's okay. Chloe sent us. We came to take you to her."

Raising tear-filled eyes to her, the woman grasped Flame's hand tightly. Her fear and disbelief showing, she whispered, "Chloe's alive? My baby is alive?"

Nodding, Flame stood and gently helped the woman to her feet. Holding a finger to her lips, Flame guided her to the door. Nico and Angel led the way out of the house, silently closing the front door behind them. When it was obvious the woman was too weak to go far, Nico gathered her in his arms and they ran swiftly back to where they left the SUV. When they were half a mile from Gentry's, Angel ordered, *Do it.*

There was the sound of glass breaking, and then nothing. After reaching the SUV, they waited for Jaxson and Rikki, then loaded up and headed to the small airport to retrieve their plane.

"He will find us," Chloe's mom whispered from where she sat huddled between Flame and Rikki in the middle of the SUV. "He told me if I ever left him, he would hunt me down and kill me."

"You don't have to worry about Gentry Samson finding you," Angel promised from the front passenger seat. Turning around to face the woman, she told her, "That bastard will never bother you again. I promise."

Her eyes widening in understanding, Chloe's mom whispered, "He's gone?"

"He's gone," Angel confirmed. Smiling gently, she said, "I'm Angel, and this is my team. Your daughter, Chloe, sent us to bring you home. You will have a new alpha. One who will protect you. One that you can trust."

Tears slipped down the woman's face as she whispered, "Layla. My name is Layla. Thank you all for helping us."

Flame slipped her hand in Layla's and silently stared out the window. RARE was a team, but they were also a family. Flame had been through the fiery depths of hell when she was held by the General, and she had set her path on revenge. But seeing the team help people like Layla and Chloe, being a part of it, was slowly helping her broken heart mend. She was not ready to set aside her vengeance, but she was slowly allowing herself to open up to new possibilities. Closing her eyes, she allowed herself to dream of a man with brown hair and gorgeous blue eyes. Bran...her mate. No, she could not give up her vengeance, not even for him.

10

It was Christmas Eve and the party was in full swing. Chase was decked out as Santa Claus and Josie was his elf. Josie had talked Chloe into taking pictures of the children on Santa's lap while Josie handed Chase their presents to give them.

One of the pack children had claimed his place on Santa's knee and was telling him what he wanted for Christmas. Santa was listening intently and giving the correct responses, but he seemed to be keeping an eye on the door. At Chloe's startled gasp, Josie swung around. With a cry, Chloe ran to the door, passing Josie the camera on her way by. In the entrance stood a small, stunning woman with long dark hair and hazel eyes. Her arms were opened wide as she waited for Chloe to reach her. Wrapping them tightly around Chloe, the woman patted her back as they both cried softly. "Mama," Chloe cried. "Oh, Mama, you are really here."

Chase gently placed the child sitting on his lap onto

the floor and rose, making his way over to the women. "Welcome to my pack, Ms. Samson."

"Please," Chloe's mother whispered as she raised her head to meet his gaze. "Call me Layla. Thank you so much for everything you have done for my daughter and me."

"You will be safe here, Layla," Chase promised. "I will protect you and Chloe." Smiling, Chase gestured to the room behind them. "Go, enjoy the festivities. Meet your pack members. You will be staying with Josie tonight, but tomorrow we will move you into your new apartment."

Smiling gratefully, Layla and Chloe made their way further into the room. They did not get far before they were surrounded by the women of the pack. Guiding Chloe and her mother over to the buffet table, they introduced themselves.

The RARE team filled the doorway once the women were gone. Nico's daughter, Lily, squealed from across the room when she saw Nico. Running to him, she launched herself into his arms when he knelt down, placing kisses all over his face. Laughing, Nico picked her up, holding her close and strolled into the room. Going to his mate, Jenna, he slid an arm around her waist and kissed her softly.

Looking around, Josie smiled. Her heart was full of joy. Phoenix and Serenity were there with Hunter. Chase's girls, Hope and Faith, were playing with their new dolls in the corner. Janie's daughter, Alayna, was dressed in a bright red dress with frills and squealing with delight at the other children in the pack. This was her family, her pack. The only thing that would make her night complete would be a visit from Ryker. She had not heard from him since he left three days before to meet with the council. As much as she missed him, she understood he had a job to do, and resisted contacting him.

Looking at her watch, Josie decided it was time to check on Storm. She was slowly recovering but seemed to be fighting it for some reason. Josie had expected more of an argument from Storm when she had forbidden her from moving around too much in the first week. However, Storm had easily surrendered and only left her bed to go to the bathroom, which she required assistance with because she was not doing the exercises Josie had given her. She did not watch television, and she refused visitors. Josie decided it was time to shove some Christmas cheer up Storm's ass. Grabbing a cup of eggnog and a piece of cake, she headed to the woman's room.

When she heard Angel's voice, Josie stopped just outside Storm's door. She did not want to eavesdrop, but Storm was her patient and Josie intended to make sure she was all right.

"It's time to leave the pity party behind, Storm," Angel said sarcastically. "Get your ass out of bed and fight back. So, you were hurt. We have all been hurt. It happens. It's time to buck up and move on."

"You don't know anything," Storm sneered. "You stand there acting like a fucking queen, but really you are just as lonely and scared as the rest of us. If you weren't, you would have let Chase claim you months ago."

"What is between Chase and I is none of your business, Storm," Angel growled.

"And I am none of your business," Storm spat back.

"That's not true," Angel argued. "I like you, Storm. I respect you. I am here tonight as your friend, but I am also here because I want to offer you a position with

RARE. I want you to work with us, be a part of our family."

In the silence that followed, Josie felt her head begin to pound. What was going on? What about Ryker? If Angel was offering Storm a position with RARE, did that mean she would offer Ryker one as well? As if reading her mind, Storm asked, "What about Ryker? I won't leave him. He's my partner."

"I have already asked Ryker to join our team," Angel told her. "He hasn't given me a response yet, but said he would after he spoke to the council."

After a moment Storm murmured, "If Ryker agrees, then I'm in. I need something different in my life, Angel," she admitted. "I can't go on like this."

"The first thing you need to do is get your ass out of that bed," Angel retorted. "Get up and take a damn shower. Then go get some cake."

Hearing Angel's voice getting nearer as she moved toward the door, Josie jumped back, guiltily clutching the drink and plate in her hand. The door opened slightly and then Angel muttered, "I can't let Chase claim me right now, Storm. My children need me. I need to concentrate on them before I can accept a mate in my life."

Opening the door fully, Angel said goodbye before walking out. Striding past Josie, she left the building without speaking to anyone else. Josie stood there in shock. If Ryker accepted a position with RARE, what would that mean for them? Why hadn't he mentioned it to her?

Pushing the thoughts out of her mind, Josie entered Storm's room and placed the goodies she had brought on the table next to the bed.

"Don't feel bad," Storm said. "He didn't mention it to either of us. I had to find out just now from Angel. If he would have told me, at least I would have been prepared when she threw out the offer."

Eyes wide, Josie asked, "How did you know what I was thinking? And that isn't the first time you have done that to me. Are you telepathic like…" Josie let the sentence trail off not wanting to give away any secrets. She was afraid she had said too much, but she was in shock.

Groaning, Storm sat up, carefully swinging her legs over the side of the bed. Running a hand through her long dark hair that hung limply down her back, she said, "Yeah, Ryker and I both are. No one else knows, though. We don't like to talk about it."

Not knowing what she thought about Ryker keeping something like that from her, Josie changed the subject. "I'm going to go start the shower. Eat your cake." Avoiding Storm's gaze, Josie went into the bathroom and turned on the water. After making sure there were towels, she went out to help Storm.

Storm was struggling to get out of bed, but when she saw Josie, she sat back down. "Ryker isn't keeping things from you, Josie. This is different. This secret was not just his to share, or he would have told you."

When Josie did not respond, Storm tried to stand up again. Fighting against the pain, sweat beaded up on Storm's forehead. Unable to stop herself, Josie moved to help her.

"Josie," Storm said, as she approached the bed. "You need to understand something." Reaching out, Storm grasped Josie's wrist with unsteady fingers. "Ryker and I have been partners for several years. He is like a brother to me." Tightening her hold on Josie's wrist, Storm continued, "If Ryker didn't tell you what we can do, it was not because he doesn't trust you. It was because he was protecting me. We made a pact twenty-eight years ago when we discovered each other's gift. We promised to keep our secrets between us. Who knows what could happen if it got out? I know Ryker wanted to tell you, Josie, but his promise to me prevented him from doing it."

Sighing, Josie sat down on the bed beside Storm. "I understand, Storm. I know about having to keep secrets. It just surprised me. First the possibility of the job with RARE, and then finding out he can read my mind."

Storm giggled, then slammed her hand over her mouth, her eyes widening in surprise. It had obviously been a long time since Storm had let go and enjoyed life. "What's so funny?" Josie demanded to distract her.

Laughing again, Storm said, "Ryker doesn't read your mind, Josie."

"He doesn't?" Josie asked in confusion. "I thought that was how it worked?"

"Ryker isn't a very strong telepath," Storm explained. "He has the gift and can speak with other telepaths, but that's all he can do. If you are a strong telepath, you can merge with others and read their thoughts and feelings. Ryker is not strong enough for that. All of your secrets are still safe."

"You keep saying Ryker isn't strong enough," Josie remarked. "You are though, aren't you?"

Nodding, Storm agreed, "Yes, I can read your thoughts if I want to, but normally I choose not to. I learned years ago to stay out of peoples' minds without an invite. Unless, of course, I am on a mission and need Intel. But I have to be near someone to read them, and body contact helps."

Josie chose to ignore the fact that if Storm wanted to, she could easily slip into her mind and see her thoughts and feelings. Gently, she pulled her wrist from the other woman's grasp. Standing up, she leaned over and helped Storm to her feet. "Let's get you in the shower, Storm. Then we can go join in the festivities down the hall for a while before bed."

After helping Storm shower and change into some red scrubs with green Christmas trees, Josie wheeled her down the hall against her protests. She knew Storm did not want to appear weak in front of everyone, but there was no way she could walk the length of the hall.

"Maybe you will get off your ass now and do your exercises," Josie said. "The only way you are going to get stronger is if you start eating and doing your exercises, Storm. You have a lot to live for." Placing a hand on Storm's shoulder, Josie leaned down to whisper, "I firmly believe your mate is out there, Storm. He is out there, and if you don't fight back and get better, where does that leave him? If you are gone, he is alone. Choose to fight, Storm. Choose to be the person you once were. Choose to be the person your mate needs."

Looking up at Josie in surprise, Storm's eyes narrowed. "You think my mate is out there? Waiting for me?"

"He's out there, Storm," Josie promised. "He's out there and is probably looking for you. Show him the woman you are. Fight for him."

Nodding in determination, Storm gritted her teeth and tightened her hold on the arms of the wheelchair.

"Fuck this. I will fight. I won't leave him out there alone somewhere."

Smiling, Josie stood back up and pushed Storm into the middle of the room full of chaotic, joyful noise. Yes, Storm would fight. Josie would make sure of it.

11

R yker let himself into Josie's home early Christmas morning, the door clicking shut quietly behind him. His meetings with the council had taken longer than expected. If he had gone just to give the details of his mission, he would have been back yesterday, but he had not gone just to give his report.

Closing his eyes, Ryker tilted his head back and inhaled deeply. The scent of his mate engulfed him and peace filled his body. Home, he was finally home. Following the scent into the living room where it was the strongest, he paused when he saw Josie asleep on the couch wrapped in a warm fleece blanket. There was a fire going in the fireplace directly in front of her.

Ryker quickly stripped off his coat placing it on the back of the couch. Making his way to her, he picked her up and laid her on the carpet in front of the fire. Josie smiled and stretched her arms above her head, a moan slipping free. The blanket slid from her body, slowly baring her silky skin. She was gloriously naked beneath the blanket. Ryker groaned, as his cock hardened painfully.

Standing, Ryker slowly unbuttoned his shirt and slid it off his shoulders, letting it fall to the ground. Undoing his belt buckle, he unbuttoned his jeans and pushed them down his legs and off. Palming his hard length, he slowly stroked it as he stared into Josie's eyes. She was so damn sexy, and she was his.

As she watched him, Josie held out her hand. Dropping to his knees beside her, Ryker clasped her hand in one of his. His other hand, he lightly traced from her ankle up her leg, over the soft flesh of her stomach and cupped one of her firm breasts. Leaning over, he kissed her softly on her lips, then nibbled his way down her neck to the breast he held. Sucking the nipple into his hot, wet mouth, he nipped lightly. Josie arched off the floor and into his mouth on a soft cry.

Letting go of Josie's breast, Ryker moved between her legs. Leaning over her, he placed his forearms on the carpet beside her head. Pressing his lips to hers, he slowly pushed deep inside her. Sliding his hands into her long dark tresses, Ryker looked deep into her mesmerizing eyes. "I love you, Josie," he whispered. Capturing her soft gasp with his mouth, he started moving. Setting a slow, steady pace, Ryker pushed in and out of his mate.

As he moved closer and closer to his own release, he felt Josie tighten around him. Feeling his fangs lengthen, Ryker picked up his pace. Josie screamed loudly, raking her claws down his back as she came, and Ryker sank his teeth into her shoulder as he burst inside her.

Breathing heavily, he licked at his mate mark.

Nuzzling her neck, he smiled when he heard her softly whisper, "I love you too, Ryker."

Leaning back, Ryker gazed at the face he was going to wake up to for the rest of his life. Smiling, he told her, "Merry Christmas, Love."

Moving to her side, Ryker wrapped Josie back up in the blanket. Holding her close, he picked her up as he stood, walking over to the couch. Sitting down, he cuddled her in his lap. "We need to talk," he said, as he gently kissed her lips.

Lightly running a finger down the side of his face, Josie murmured. "I probably already know everything you want to talk about."

"Really?" he asked curiously. Nipping lightly at her earlobe he whispered, "Tell me."

"Well," she responded, as she snuggled deeper into his chest, "I know that you are telepathic. You can speak with others, but are unable to read their minds. Storm explained that you couldn't tell me because you had promised her years ago not to say anything."

"She's right," Ryker agreed as he rubbed his chin over the top of her head. "We made a pact and I could not break it. But, I was going to talk to her about making an exception. I want to know everything there is to know about you, Josie, and I want to tell you everything about me."

Nodding, Josie whispered, "I was hurt at first that you didn't tell me. I thought you didn't trust me. But I've had time to think about it, and I know you would have told me if you could have."

God, he loved this woman, Ryker thought, stroking a hand down her thigh. It happened quickly, but that was the way with mates. There was a bond that snapped into place at mating and love normally followed.

"And I know Angel offered you a job with RARE," Josie continued. "I heard her tell Storm last night when she offered her a job."

Tilting her head up so he could watch her expression, Ryker asked, "And how do you feel about that?"

"I want you to be happy, Ryker. I will back whatever decision you make. I will go where ever you go. I love you and want to be with you."

Grinning, Ryker kissed her lips, mapping her mouth with his tongue. Pulling back finally, he told her, "I met with the council yesterday. I have served them well for several years. They are letting me go, Josie. And they are letting Storm go, as well, if she is ready to move on. I also talked to Chase. Both Storm and I have the option of joining either the White River Wolf pack or accepting Angel as our Alpha. I have chosen to work with RARE, so I have accepted Angel. I will be living here with you in the White River compound, though. Chase has approved everything."

Squealing excitedly, Josie threw her arms around Ryker, hugging him close. "Thank you, Ryker. Thank you so much," she exclaimed. "I didn't want to leave. I have so many people here that need me. But for you, I would have."

"Well now you don't have to make that decision." Gathering her close, Ryker stood and carried her out of the living room and up the stairs to her bedroom. Seeing the other bedroom door closed, he raised his eyebrows. Blushing, Josie whispered, "Chloe and her mom are here. They are sleeping."

A wicked grin stretching across his face, Ryker chuckled, "I doubt that with the way you were screaming downstairs."

He laughed as Josie's eyes widened in horror. Walking into their bedroom, he kicked the door shut behind him. Laying her on the bed, he growled, "Let's see if I can make you scream again."

Laughing, a pretty blush spreading from her cheeks down, Josie wrapped her arms tightly around Ryker's neck pulling him on top of her. "Merry Christmas, Mate," she whispered before his mouth claimed hers.

Make sure and visit my website for information on all of my books, and to sign up for my Newsletter where you will receive all of the latest information on new releases, sales, and more!

Website: **http://www.dawnsullivanauthor.com/**

I would love to have you join my reader's group, Author Dawn Sullivan's RARE Rebels, so that we can hang out and chat, and where you will also get sneak peeks of cover reveals, read excerpts before anyone else, and more!

https://www.facebook.com/groups/AuthorDawnSullivan sRebelReaders/

Dawn Sullivan

ABOUT THE AUTHOR

Dawn Sullivan has a wonderful, supportive husband, and three beautiful children. She enjoys spending time with them, which normally involves some baseball, shooting hoops, taking walks, watching movies, and reading.

Her passion for reading began at a very young age and only grew over time. Whether she was bringing home a book from the library, or sneaking one of her mother's romance novels to read by the light in the hallway when she was supposed to be sleeping, Dawn always had a book. She reads several different genres and subgenres, but Paranormal Romance and Romantic Suspense are her favorites.

Dawn has always made up stories of her own, and finally decided to start sharing them with others. She hopes everyone enjoys reading them as much as she enjoys writing them.

facebook.com/dawnsullivanauthor

twitter.com/dawn_author

instagram.com/dawn_sullivan_author

Made in the USA
Coppell, TX
05 July 2024

34300696R00056